Louise

All the **Fun Winter Things**

by Erica S. Perl

illustrated by Chris Chatterton

Penguin Workshop

PENGUIN WORKSHOP
An Imprint of Penguin Random House LLC, New York

Text copyright © 2019 by Erica S. Perl. Illustrations copyright © 2019 by Penguin Random House LLC. All rights reserved. Published by Penguin Workshop, an imprint of Penguin Random House LLC, New York. PENGUIN and PENGUIN WORKSHOP are trademarks of Penguin Books Ltd, and the W colophon is a registered trademark of Penguin Random House LLC. Manufactured in China.

Visit us online at www.penguinrandomhouse.com.

Library of Congress Cataloging-in-Publication Data is available upon request.

ISBN 9781524790486 (paperback)   10 9 8 7 6 5 4 3 2 1
ISBN 9781524790493 (library binding)   10 9 8 7 6 5 4 3 2 1

To Franny, for arriving in winter and making life considerably more fun—ESP

Chapter One

"Arnold, look!" said Louise.

She skidded to a stop, then twirled in place.

"Ta-da! The pond is frozen. Come sliding with me!"

"I can't," said Arnold. "When it gets cold, it's time for me to hibernate. You know about hibernating, right? It's like taking a long winter nap."

"Well, what about tomorrow?" asked Louise.

Arnold shook his head. "I'll be asleep until spring."

"Until *spring*?" Louise stared at Arnold. "What kind of hibernating is *that*?"

Arnold shrugged. "Regular hibernating?"

"Regular for bears, maybe," said Louise. "Not for chipmunks."

"Chipmunks hibernate?" asked Arnold.

He found it hard to believe.

Louise couldn't sit still for a few minutes, let alone sleep for months.

"Of course we hibernate!" said Louise. "Just not like *that*. If we did, we'd miss all the fun winter things."

Arnold had never thought about that.

He didn't want to miss all the fun winter things.

"Hey, I have an idea," said Louise. "Why don't you try being a chipmunk?"

"I wish

I could,"

said Arnold.

"Did you

say *wish*?

Good thing

I brought my magic wand."

Louise picked it up and

waved it in the air.

"Alakazam, alakazunk. You

are now a Junior Chipmunk!"

"That's nice, Louise, but—"

"Shhhh!" said Louise. "Watch

and learn, Junior Chipmunk."

8

Chapter Two

"Follow me, Junior

Chipmunk!" called Louise.

Arnold did as he was told.

After a hike along the edge

of the pond, Louise paused.

"Now, it's time to hibernate like a chipmunk. Ready? One. Two. Three. Sleep!"

"Wait, what?" asked Arnold.

"Hibernate," said Louise. "You know. Close your eyes. Go to sleep."

13

"Here?" Arnold looked around. "It doesn't look very comfortable."

"Chipmunks love to try new things," said Louise.

"Fine," said Arnold.

He lay down on the ground and closed his eyes.

Within moments he was drifting off to—

"Junior Chipmunk, wake up!"

14

"Huh, what?" Arnold sat up
and rubbed his eyes.

"Ice sliding time,"
announced Louise.

"Sliding? But I thought we
were hibernating."

15

Louise shook her head.

"We just did that, silly!"

"But we only slept for a few minutes. I'm still sleepy."

"Don't worry, we'll hibernate more later. First—ice sliding!"

Arnold stumbled to his feet.

"I'm not sure I'm awake enough for ice sliding," he told Louise.

"Just one lap around the pond," she said.

"Okay," agreed Arnold. "One lap. Then: more sleep."

"Deal," said Louise.

Chapter Three

One lap led to another.

And another.

And another.

Which led to ice

dancing,

19

ice hockey, and even some

ice fishing.

Finally, they went back to Arnold's house.

Arnold sank into his favorite chair.

"Sleeping time?" he asked.

"Right! Time for more hibernating," said Louise. "One. Two. Three. Sleep!"

Arnold closed his eyes.

"Aaaaand . . . wake up!" said Louise.

23

Arnold opened his eyes.

"Sledding time," announced

Louise.

24

"Louise, I didn't even fall

asleep yet."

"It's okay, Junior Chipmunk.

We'll sleep more later. We need to do all the fun winter things!"

Arnold really wanted to sleep more *now*.

But he didn't want to miss any of the fun winter things.

"Just one run," said Louise.

"One run," agreed Arnold. "And then a lot more sleep."

"Deal," said Louise.

26

27

Chapter Four

One run led to another.

And another.

And another.

One jump—*whee!*

Led to one bump—*whoa!*

Led to one crash landing—

nooooo!

Which led to many snow angels, one snow chipmunk, and one glorious snowball battle.

Finally, they returned to

Arnold's house.

Arnold lay down on the floor.

"Sleep!" he said. "A good long sleep this time. Right? You promised!"

"Okay, no problem," said
Louise. "Ready? One. Two.
Three. Sleep!"

Arnold smiled sleepily.

"Aaaaand . . . !"

"No!" yelled Arnold.

"What's wrong?" asked Louise.

"I'm not ready," said Arnold. "Please let me sleep."

"But there are still so many fun winter things to do!"

"Can't. Too sleepy."

"Junior Chipmunk, you are leaving me no choice," said Louise. "If you don't get up, I'm going to have to alakazam you back!"

Arnold stayed put.

Louise stared at him. "Just so you know, if I undo it, I can't *un*-undo it."

"Okay," said Arnold.

Louise raised her wand.

"Alakazam, alakazen. You are now a bear again."

"So, I guess that's that," said Arnold.

"Don't feel bad," said Louise. "Not everyone is meant to be a chipmunk."

She gave Arnold a hug and went on her way.

After Louise left, Arnold climbed into his bed.

He closed his eyes.

He breathed a sigh of relief.

Ahhhhhhh.

His home was cozy, warm,

and quiet.

Very quiet.

Pleasingly quiet.

No-Louise-ing-ly quiet.

Too quiet?

Chapter Five

"Arnold," said Louise. "What are you doing here?"

Arnold shrugged. "I think I forgot how to be a bear."

"But you can't be a

chipmunk, Arnold. I already alakazammed you back."

"I know," said Arnold. "I just don't want to spend the winter without you."

"I don't want to spend the winter without you, either!" Louise replied.

"Any chance you want to try being a bear?" suggested Arnold.

Louise laughed. "Good one," she said.

"Then I don't know what to do," said Arnold.

"Hmm," said Louise. "This is a problem."

She sat down with Arnold outside and they both tried to think.

Finally, Louise said, "Can you stay awake just a little longer?"

Arnold nodded.

Louise walked Arnold back to his house.

They built a fire in his woodstove.

Then, they sat in front of it and read books.

One book led to another.

And another.

"One more?"

And another.

Which led to four songs, several card games, and two delicious mugs of piping-hot cocoa.

Finally, the fire burned down to glowing embers.

Arnold let out a bear-size *yaaaaaawn.*

Then, Louise tucked Arnold into bed.

"I'm sorry, Louise," said Arnold. "I really wanted to stay awake for all the fun winter things."

"But you already did," said Louise.

Arnold looked at her in surprise. "I did?"

Louise nodded. "Reading

and playing indoors are the last fun winter things I know. So, now we've done all the fun winter things. Except for one."

"What's that?" asked Arnold.

Louise smiled. "Checking on you."

"You'll check on me while I'm asleep?" asked Arnold.

"All the time," Louise promised. "When you wake

up, it will be spring. And
then we'll do all the fun
spring things together.
Okay, Arnold?"

Arnold did not answer.

He was already asleep.

"Happy hibernating,
Arnold," whispered Louise.

Arnold and Louise

Follow these furry
friends on more
adventures!

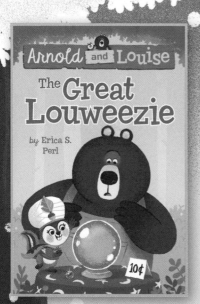

Arnold and Louise

The Great Louweezie

by Erica S. Perl

10¢

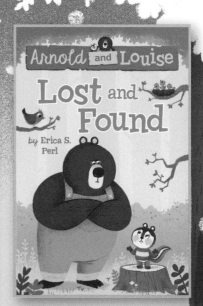

Arnold and Louise

Lost and Found

by Erica S. Perl

Arnold and Louise

Happy Fell

by Erica S. Perl